In Praise of

"I have just read **Q-23** with pleasu   d
specific—the creation of 'Hair B   :t
in fiction, putting me in mind of   i's
'Filboid Studge.' My congratulati   :h
my wish that the novel finds ma:

    —**Paul E. Theroux**, author of _. _____ _____ _____, _The Old_
        Patagonian Express, The Mosquito Coast, Dark Star Safari, and other
        bestselling books

"What's in a name? Great writing has long been associated with the
Theroux name. Paul R. Theroux's novel joins the ranks of Theroxs
whose writing is well worth reading. The title of Paul Theroux's new
novel is a very clever play on words. But unlike many books adorned
with clever titles, the story embedded in **_Q-23: A Novel of Espionage
and Racqueteering_** is as clever as the title. I was hooked from the
get-go."

    —**Kenneth G. Elzinga, Ph.D.**, author of _Murder at the Margin,_
        The Fatal Equilibrium, and _A Deadly Indifference_

"I have found **Q-23** fascinating. I could not put it down and I have taken it
everywhere. Paul Theroux has one vivid imagination and yet everything
is so plausible. I have really enjoyed the story, especially having been
myself in healthcare both in business and government. The book is short
as are the chapters, a great formula for a quick, easy, informative and
interesting read. Highly recommended!"

    —**Don M. Newman**, former Undersecretary, U.S. Department of
        Health and Human Services; author, _Newman's Musings: Reflections
        of a Life_

A NOVEL OF ESPIONAGE AND RACQUETEERING

PAUL R. THEROUX

LibertyTree Press

Oakland, California

Q-23: A Novel of Espionage and Racqueteering

Copyright © 2013 by LibertyTree Press

LibertyTree Press
100 Swan Way, Oakland, CA 94621-1428
Telephone: 510-568-6047
Fax: 510-568-6040
Email: info@libertytree.com
Website: www.libertytree.com

ISBN 978-0-9886556-0-7
Library of Congress Cataloging-in-Publication Data Available

Cover Design: Keith Criss
Illustrations by Wythe Bowart
Interior Design and Composition by Jaad Book Design

To my children,
David, Gary, and Linda

Contents

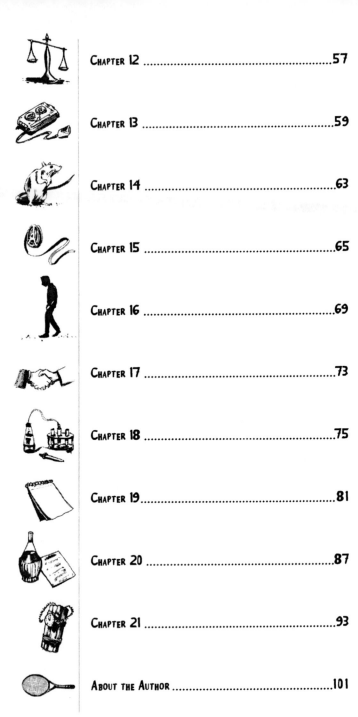

Chapter 1

KURT STRONG knew something was bothering his opponent. Usually, Roger Pate extended himself to maximum effort and concentration—but not this evening.

After scores of 6–2 and 6–1, Kurt started around the tennis net to change sides for the third set, when Roger startled him with, "Let's call it enough. I'm sorry, Kurt, but I'm way off somewhere."

"Okay," Kurt conceded grudgingly. He disliked attaining what seemed like only half a workout, and they had twenty-five minutes remaining of the one and a half hours they had reserved at the indoor tennis center. In the three years they had been pounding a ball at each other, Kurt couldn't remember Roger not wanting to play until the last minute. In fact, that was one reason they had such good matches; they both went all out to win, and neither wanted to give up a point without a struggle.

Roger seemed to sense the question in his friend's mind. "You're right, Kurt. I've got a problem that's bugging me. Let's go for a beer, and I'll tell you about it."

Infrequently, after a game at the indoor tennis center, they dropped by the Side Door Bar and Grill. Infrequently because Roger wanted to get home to his wife and two young kids. Kurt was single, a bit younger at twenty-six, and he would have preferred a visit to the Side Door Bar and Grill follow each tennis session. After three of their normally hot sets of tennis, it was the time he most enjoyed a cold draft beer. Also, he liked Roger, who reminded him of a big friendly dog with his enthusiasm and excitability. A chemist, Roger was the chemical research manager at a sizeable conglomerate—Benson & Co., just outside of Chicago.

After taking a long satisfying drink from the frosted mug in front of him, Kurt prompted, "Well, what's this problem you were talking about?"

Roger didn't respond immediately. His usually friendly face looked deadly serious, and he studied Kurt's eyes for a moment. Finally he blurted out, "Hell, I shouldn't be telling you my troubles. It's just that I'm up against something that has me up a tree, and I don't know what to do." He paused.

Trying to be helpful, Kurt offered, "Is it trouble at home?"

"No, everything is fine at home. It's at work. They're trying to pull something I don't like. In fact, they've already done it." He paused again, scowling intently into his half-empty mug of beer, as if the problem was hiding somewhere in the light-brown liquid. His six foot two, two hundred-pound body was tautly hunched in the secluded booth they had selected in the nearly empty tavern. Kurt waited patiently until Roger continued. "I know you have a law degree, and while you're not in active practice, maybe you can give me some free legal advice." He smiled briefly, without any mirth. "The lab project I've been working on for the past year was an improved shaving cream, one that would soften the beard so a razor blade would cut through whiskers like they were made of soft butter. About four months ago, it happened." Roger's eyes seemed to ignite as he looked up, recalling the thrill of success. "I finally came up with a combination that did just what we wanted. Even a relatively dull razor blade would produce a clean shave, with no stress or strain on the face."

"Sounds great," Kurt inserted.

"Yeah, if I had let it go at that—but I had to go and fuss with it some more." Roger's face screwed itself into a wry, disgusted expression. "If I had just quit while I was ahead, everything would be okay. Soly was happy as a lark. He's my boss. So I should have let it lay, but I figured I could make it even better." He paused and drained his beer mug.

"I'll get some more beer," Kurt offered, as he picked up the two mugs and stepped up to the bar.

With the refills in front of them, Roger continued. "Well, anyway, I kept adding more and more of this one ingredient. It's a new kind of softener I found. Finally, I had it. Formula Q-23 not only softened the whiskers, *it actually made them disappear!* What do you think of that?" he demanded.

"Come on," Kurt laughed. "What do you mean, *disappear*? Sounds like you invented vanishing cream."

"Well, in a way it is, 'cause it does make whiskers vanish. That's the beauty of it." Roger was enthusiastic. "It seems to affect only hair. Doesn't hurt the skin at all. I tested it on myself—no problems. It removes the hair all the way down to and including the roots. That's the biggie; it removes the roots. Until now, the only hair-removal method that removed the hair root, or hair bulb, was electrolysis, and that method has its drawbacks, including some pit-like scarring, time involved, and high costs. There have been some other cream-type hair removers, but they don't compare with Q-23. It's permanent hair removal with one application."

"Wow! Sounds like you really have something. You and your company should be happy. So what's the problem?"

"The problem is that Benson & Co. is a conglomerate. When I brought Q-23 to Soly, my boss, he was amazed, but he didn't seem pleased. He told me to keep it quiet. About a week later, I pinned him down. It seems our big moneymaker is razors, razor blades, and everything else that goes with shaving. Soly says he discussed my formula with our president, and they decided to do nothing with Q-23. Just bottle it up. The biggest thing I have ever come up with, and they want to stifle it."

The resentment and distress showed on Roger's face. He had worked at Benson & Co. for eight years now, since graduating from college. Benson & Co. had previously used outside chemical labs, but with Roger, they could handle special chemical research at a lower cost and with a better chance of keeping any new developments or products secret. He had his own small laboratory and office and reported directly to Sylvester (Soly) Claybourne, Vice President of Research and Development.

Kurt stared at Roger for a moment. "You mean to tell me they're not going to market an obvious winner like that?"

"That's right. Soly told me that 90 percent of our profits come from shaving products, and if nobody shaved it could blow most of those profits away. Benson & Co. has millions of dollars in shaving inventory, and even more millions in plants and expensive equipment. If Q-23 caught on, it could make all this obsolete. Anyway, Soly told me I had to think like management about the good of the company—and keep it secret. Well, I've always tried to be a good company man, always followed the rules, but this is different."

"What do you mean, different?" asked Kurt.

"Well, first of all, it's an important discovery—sort of a medical breakthrough—something that a researcher like me may come across only once in a lifetime. So from a personal standpoint, it's really important to me—as a person, a chemist, and a researcher—to not keep it bottled up. Secondly, I feel I have a duty to the public not to hide a product like this. This may sound like I'm trying to be noble, but it's not like that. Just think of the hundreds of millions of men who have to go through the bother of shaving every day, to say nothing about the time and expense involved. One application of Q-23 and you're through with shaving. I know. A month ago I gave myself the treatment, and I haven't shaved since. Here, feel my face," he said as he leaned forward and jutted out his chin.

Kurt ran his hand over Roger's chin and neck, and, with some awe in his voice, said, "Smooth as a baby's behind. Say, I suppose it would work on women, too."

"Sure it would," enthused Roger. "You'd be amazed at the number of women customers our division has. Even with the feminist movement, women want to be feminine, and that means no hair on most parts of the body. In fact, we probably would have as many, if not more, women customers for Q-23 than men."

"You've convinced me," Kurt admitted. "But why are you talking to me? Not that I'm not interested, but I don't see how I can help you."

"Maybe you can't," Roger agreed. "But I had to tell someone. I haven't even told my wife about it. I think she suspects something's going on, but so far I've honored our company's policy and position by not talking to anyone till now. Now four of us know about it: Soly, Mr. Benson, you, and me. I guess I'm telling you partly because I consider you one of my best friends, but also because I thought you might give me some help from a legal standpoint, regarding what is right in a case such as this or what I should do."

Kurt pondered a moment. "Off the cuff, I'd have to say you are stuck with your boss's position. Since your president reportedly agrees with him, this seems to eliminate going over your boss's head."

"I know," Roger scowled. "I've been thinking about going to the chairman of the board, but he's semi-retired, and I'm not sure I could get in to see him, anyway. Probably I'd just end up without a job."

"I doubt that," mused Kurt. "It seems to me you have a pretty strong hand. If they fired you, you could make this public, or go to a competitor, or start your own business. Of course, there could be legal problems, since you discovered this while working for Benson & Co. I doubt they would fire you, though, even if they wanted to. If you really want to fight this, why don't you confront your boss again, and try to obtain a hearing with your president, so you can explain your feelings firsthand."

"Maybe I should," Roger admitted. "I have to do something. This keeps bothering me so much, I can't do anything else right."

"Yeah, I noticed that on the tennis court," smiled Kurt. "I like to beat you, but not that easily."

"I was pretty bad, wasn't I?" agreed Roger sheepishly, as he looked at his watch. "I'd better get going or my wife will get even more suspicious about what is going on."

Kurt killed off his beer, and as they were walking out to their respective cars, added, "Look, Roger, let me know how this goes. If you get your day in court with your president and the issue is not resolved, let me know and let's talk further. We'll come up with something."

"Okay. I feel better already. I'll call you later this week. Thanks, Kurt."

On the way back to his bachelor's apartment, Kurt thought about Roger's plight. There must be more to the story. He couldn't imagine a big outfit like Benson & Co. trying to suppress a product like the one Roger had described. Yet Kurt had known Roger for several years, and he doubted Roger was feeding him a line or was greatly exaggerating the facts. While Benson & Co. was a large, well-respected company, it could be that one or two persons in management might pigeonhole a potential product like this for one reason or another, rightly or wrongly.

Kurt was trained and experienced in being analytical. When he had finished law school, he found he had little desire to take up the profession, even though he had been offered a start with a well-known law firm in Chicago. Instead, he did some investigative work, first with an insurance company and then with a private investigating firm. Then, just two years ago, he established his own firm, Strong Consulting and Investigating Service. Business had developed slowly the first year, but was doing well now, partly due to former contacts with the insurance industry and partly due to some hard work and the high degree of confidence and competence he displayed with other people. Also, his lean dark good looks and a six-foot athletic frame were not a handicap. The volume of business had developed so much that he had hired a young high school graduate named Ray Grayson. Ray was a happy-go-lucky youth who handled some routine outside work, but whose main jobs were to answer the phone when Kurt was out and to keep the office paperwork from becoming too much of a fire hazard.

Kurt was still thinking about Roger's problem when he was lying in bed that night, but he saw no easy solution. He dismissed the matter from his mind, turned on his side, and went to sleep.

CHAPTER 2

IN HIS LITTLE office in his laboratory at Benson & Co. the next morning, Roger Pate waited until mid-morning before he pushed 207 on the intercom. "This is Roger Pate. I'd like to see Soly," he said to Betty. Roger knew that Betty disliked anyone referring to her boss as "Soly." She considered it disrespectful, considering that Mr. Claybourne was a vice president, but Roger was feeling a bit belligerent.

"I'll see if Mr. Claybourne can fit you in," she retorted coldly. "I'll call you back later."

An hour later, Roger received word from Betty. "Mr. Claybourne has a very busy schedule, but he can see you at 3:45 p.m. this afternoon."

Sylvester Claybourne had been with Benson & Co. for about five years. He was a small handsome man in his late forties, with a full head of dark hair, just beginning to be tinged with gray. In fact, his hair was somewhat of an obsession with him. He had a nervous habit of whipping out a pocket comb to run through his hair. Then he would pat his hair on the sides to fluff it up on top. He was very ambitious, and felt that as vice president of research and development, he was in a good spot to promote his accomplishments and move up in the organization. The position of executive vice president was currently open. However, there were several other vice-presidents in Benson & Co., and Sylvester was determined to beat them out. Much depended on pleasing Mr. Benson Jr., President, who had absolute control, through stock ownership—his own, plus the Benson family's.

Roger walked in to Sylvester's relatively plush office promptly at 3:45 p.m. and was greeted with, "I have a meeting at four o'clock. What's on your mind, Roger?"

"It's Q-23. I still—" began Roger.

"Hold on, Roger." The vice president held up a hand like a traffic cop. "I told you our position on Q-23. We must defer any further action at this time. Maybe next year, if conditions are right. Now, was there anything else you wanted to see me about?"

"Can't we at least try testing—""

"Now look, Roger." The irritation showed on Sylvester's face and in his voice. Unconsciously, he pulled out his comb and passed it rapidly through his hair. "We've been through this, and it's settled. Your Q-23 is deferred for the present." Then his attitude abruptly changed to a confidential tone, as he walked around his desk and put a friendly hand on Roger's arm.

"Look, Roger. This is a corporate decision for the good of the organization and, therefore, for the good of all of us. Just relax. We all appreciate the value of the work you've done and the potential of Q-23, and we may be able to do something with it next year, or the following year when our profits are not dependent on the razor division. But right now, it would be disastrous. You have plenty to do with your other projects, so just get back to your lab and keep up the good work."

Roger felt trapped, and thought maybe he should forget it for now. But then a surge of rebellion swept over him. He stepped away from the vice president, turned to face him, and blurted out, "I'd like to talk to the president."

The irritation that Sylvester had been trying to hide now returned. "Damn it, Roger, you're going too far." The comb again came out of his pocket and passed through his luxuriant locks. "You're just going to cause both of us a lot of trouble. I advise you to just get back to your lab."

However, Roger was too riled up to be put off. So he squared his shoulders, looked Sylvester directly in the eye, and repeated his request flatly.

"Soly, I request an audience with our president, Mr. Benson Jr." He added, "Or with Mr. Benson Sr., Chairman of the Board." They glared at each other, Roger being at least six inches taller than his boss.

Finally, Sylvester reluctantly said, "All right, Roger, I'll see what I can do."

Everyone in the company knew that Benson & Co. officially had an open-door policy. At the annual company picnic outing, Mr. Benson Sr. referred to their open-door policy every year during his off-the-cuff talk to the gathered employees. This customarily occurred sandwiched in between the eating and the games. He would say something like "If any of you feel you want to talk personally to me, or to Junior, about anything having to do with our business, just pass the word through your supervisor."

Some of the supervisors as well as higher management persons winced every time Mr. Benson Sr. made these remarks, although very few employees ever took advantage of the open-door policy. It was generally accepted that you were taking a big chance of promoting disfavor with all supervisors and management persons— other than Mr. Benson Sr.—if you asked to see either Mr. Benson Sr., or Mr. Benson Jr. Such disfavor could show up in many unprovable ways—some insignificant and some significant, the most insidious being a less favorable annual rating by your supervisor, which would result in less money in future salary considerations. Mr. Benson Sr. was now semiretired. He had built the company, and during its early years he knew every employee personally. He was a naturally gregarious man, and was generally liked by everyone. However, his only son did not inherit this trait, and was much more withdrawn. Mr. Benson Jr. sometimes tried to fake it and emulate his father, but it never came across as sincere. He felt much more comfortable working on the company's financial aspects. Actually, he hated the open-door policy, and took an immediate dislike to anyone who took advantage of it.

When Sylvester notified Mr. Benson Jr. that Roger Pate had asked for an audience under the open-door policy regarding Q-23, Mr. Benson Jr. closed his eyes in simulated pain. "Can't you keep him out of my hair, Soly? I know what he wants, and I can't give it to him. I don't want to see Roger Pate. We have to think about what is best for the whole company. Soly, I'm going to leave it in your hands to take care of this. I just don't want to see him."

"He is very insistent," said Soly.

"Well, Soly, I consider it part of your job to protect me from such things. I'm sure you'll find a way to handle it." Mr. Benson hesitated a moment, then continued as if he were switching to a separate item, but Soly got the connection loud and clear, as he nervously pulled out his comb and passed it through his hair.

"By the way, Soly, on a more important subject, it's almost time to start annual performance evaluations and salary considerations. Get back to me next week with your evaluations and salary suggestions for your people. I'll be working on yours and those of the other officers in the meantime."

Sylvester Claybourne walked slowly back to his office. He kept thinking about the five years he had put in with Benson & Co. He felt he had done an outstanding job as head of Research and Development, but he still did not feel secure, especially not about his chances at that open executive vice president spot. He realized the feelings were due to his being so dependent on the favorable approval of Mr. Benson Jr. Back at his office, he sat down at his desk, but did not dig into the stack of papers there. Instead, he sat quietly, thinking, "The most important thing I have to do is find a solution to this problem with Roger Pate. That bastard, Junior, has dumped it into my lap, and if I don't handle it . . ." He reached into the center drawer of his desk, pulled out a pad of yellow paper, and wrote:

Problem: Roger Pate and Q-23

Below that he wrote:

Possible Solutions:
1. Convince Roger to drop it
2. Pay Roger to drop it
3. Eliminate Roger

He tried to think of other possibilities, but nothing else made any sense, so he kept coming back to these three possible solutions to his problem. He was not optimistic about number one, "Convince Roger to drop it," but felt it was worth another try; perhaps he should threaten to fire Roger. Regarding number two, "Pay Roger to drop it," he told himself it would be worth considerable money if Roger would go for it. The thought of an outright bribe didn't bother Sylvester, but he muttered to himself, "That sanctimonious Roger Pate would act offended." He could assure Roger of an "outstanding" performance rating in the upcoming annual performance evaluations, which would mean a big salary increase. It might work. Possible solution number three, "Eliminate Roger," would be a last resort, but if necessary, a call made to a contact he knew, from a life he had put behind him, could be made.

Sylvester started to feel better, as he always did when his course of action had been decided. He slipped the yellow pad back into his desk and locked the drawer. Then he punched Roger's intercom number.

CHAPTER 3

WHEN ROGER came into Sylvester's office later that day, the vice president was on his best behavior, and exuded friendship and charm.

"Well, Roger, I talked to Mr. Benson Jr. like you wanted. He wanted me to express his gratitude to you for the terrific job you've done in developing Q-23, as well as for the other outstanding work you've done."

"I appreciate that," Roger acknowledged warily.

"Mr. Benson Jr. also feels that Q-23 could develop into one of our major product lines in the future. Now, just when that will happen isn't clear at this time. We need to do more testing of the product to make sure it works right. You know we wouldn't want to rush into something like this before we are certain there are no side effects. Also, we need to determine whether the results are permanent hair removal, or just temporary. Therefore, Roger, just keep up with your testing, and we'll talk about it again later in the year. In the meantime, it's important to keep all this confidential among the three of us—Mr. Benson Jr., you, and myself."

Roger did not respond to the beaming smile on Sylvester's face. Instead, he responded with, "I see; it's still to be bottled up. As you know, I've already tested it on myself, and it *is* permanent, or at least for a month or so, with no side effects. So what about my request for a meeting with Mr. Benson?" Roger couldn't help but add, "Or is this open-door policy the joke that some employees say it is?"

The smile faded from the vice president's face, and he replied tersely, "Look, Roger, you're only hurting yourself with this attitude. Remember you have a good position here at Benson & Co. for a person of your age and experience. If you cooperate and keep your nose clean, you can go higher in this organization. I don't mind telling you that I hope to move up one of these days, and that will leave an opening in my spot that perhaps you can fill. So don't rock the boat, or you might fall out."

"If you're hinting that I might get fired, I don't care anymore. Q-23 is too important to me."

Sylvester paused, and thought about the yellow paper in his desk drawer. It was no surprise to him that possible solution number one (convince Roger to drop it) did not work, but at least he had tried. Now was the time to switch to possible solution number two (pay Roger to drop it).

"Now, Roger, don't get me wrong. I didn't mean you might get fired. I'm talking about the rosy future you could have here at Benson & Co. In fact, due to the excellent job you've done with Q-23, and your other great work, I've been planning to give you a performance rating of 'outstanding.' You know what that means—a salary increase of at least 15 percent. I bet you and your wife could use that extra 15 percent."

Roger was thinking rapidly. It looked like Soly was really on the spot, the way he was squirming. He wondered how far he could go, and how far Soly would go. "That 15 percent salary increase sure sounds good. We could use the extra money."

Claybourne started to congratulate himself, until Roger continued with, "But what about a promotion, and a bonus?"

Inside, Sylvester started to boil, and he automatically reached for his comb to pass through his perfectly groomed hair. He was able to control his voice with, "Well, I don't know, Roger, there's no spot right now for a promotion, but like I said, if things go right for me, you might end up in my position before long. Regarding a bonus, I might be able to arrange a special merit bonus for you. It would have to be kept confidential so other employees wouldn't get jealous, wondering why you were deserving of a bonus. We can't tell them about Q-23 yet. By the way, I trust you have not told your wife or anyone else about Q-23?"

"Of course I haven't told my wife; it would be in violation of company policy." Roger evaded fully answering the question. He didn't want to lie, but he couldn't help recalling his discussion with Kurt Strong. So he quickly switched back to the bonus subject. "How much bonus are you talking about, and when?"

Claybourne knew he was being taken advantage of by his subordinate, and he hated Roger for it. He slowly responded with, "I would think a few thousand dollars, and within a few weeks."

Roger, knowing he was in the driver's seat, prodded further with, "You say a few thousand. That's too vague. How about something more specific—like ten thousand dollars."

Sylvester knew that Benson & Co., and specifically Mr. Benson Jr., would not go for this bonus stuff, so it meant that Sylvester would need to pay it out of his own pocket, and to do that he would need to cash in some of the shares of stock he had accumulated over the past years. Before responding, his hand again pulled out his comb and nervously ran it through his already well-combed hair. Finally he conceded, "Okay, Roger, we'll make it ten thousand dollars. Do we have an agreement?"

Roger felt he had now determined how far his boss would go, so he drew himself up to his full six feet, two inches, and stated flatly, "Soly, I think the whole deal stinks, and I still want to see Mr. Benson Jr. or Mr. Benson Sr."

With that, Roger wheeled about and stalked out of Sylvester's office.

Sylvester sat fuming at his desk, until finally his anger boiled up, and he exploded with, "Bastard!" He unlocked his desk drawer, took out the yellow pad of paper, and contemplated his next step. Roger would not listen to reason, so Sylvester drew a line through "Convince Roger to drop it." Roger was just egging him on about a payment, so a line was drawn through "Pay Roger to drop it." Sylvester stared at "Eliminate Roger." Then, methodically, he tore off the top sheet from the pad, picked up a pack of matches, lighted one, held it to the paper, and tossed the burning paper into a large ashtray on his desk.

CHAPTER 4

ROGER WENT through the motions in his laboratory for the rest of the week, doing some routine work on duties that did not involve Q-23. He carefully purged his files of any material pertaining to Q-23, although he had no clear idea why. It just seemed advisable to him that if something happened, he should not leave any details about his discovery for others to find.

On Friday afternoon, Roger left work a bit earlier than usual to catch the 5:10 p.m. commuter train. He did not notice upon leaving the office that a man began following him. Aboard the train, Roger paid no attention to the man who boarded shortly after him and sat down a few seats back of him. Roger's thoughts were mostly still clogged up with Q-23, Benson & Co., and Soly.

However, when Roger reached his station and stepped off the train, he finally sensed the presence and scrutiny of the man who followed closely behind him.

The man was slightly shorter than Roger, had thin, dark features, and carried a long black umbrella, even though there had been no hint of rain recently.

Roger's wife normally picked him up at the station, but that was when he took the next train, coming in half an hour later. The one phone booth at the station was being used, so Roger headed for the Town Tavern across the street. He noticed the thin-featured man with the umbrella pretend to be absorbed in looking at a poster. Roger entered the tavern and went to the public phone booth at the rear. As he dialed his home phone number, he kept an eye on the door and was not surprised when the man entered, then looked around until his eyes met Roger's. There was no answer at Roger's home. As Roger hung up, the man strolled over and greeted Roger with a smile and, "Say, don't I know you? You look like some-one I used to know."

Roger hesitated. He was sure he had never met this man before, but he was curious about what the guy was up to, so he said, "I don't think so, but you do look familiar."

"Yeah, that's what I thought. How about me buying you a drink, and maybe we can remember where we met before. Here's a table over here. My name is Dan Grover." His handshake was strong and friendly, but Roger noticed that Dan did not ask his name, or seem to notice that it was not offered.

Dan turned out to be quite loquacious, without really saying anything, as he ordered drinks and talked a blue streak. When the drinks arrived, Roger took a sip, and then excused himself to try the phone again. In the bar mirror, he thought he saw Dan pick up the drink across the table and then replace it. There was still no answer at home. Roger was tempted not to return to the table, but he did, with some apprehension. He pretended to drink, but merely wet his lips. His chemist background confirmed that his drink had been doctored. It smelled and tasted like a potent drug that acts as an opiate, or strong sedative. When his companion, in turn, went to make a phone call to "a friend," Roger spilled most of his drink on the floor, without anyone noticing. After Dan returned, and wanting to see what would happen, Roger started to feign drowsiness. Dan watched him closely.

"Since you can't get ahold of your wife, I'll give you a ride home, ol' buddy," Dan offered as he helped Roger up and guided him to the door. "I got hold of my friend, who should be picking me up about now." True enough, outside, a big black car appeared almost magically, driven by another man.

As Dan started to herd him into the backseat, Roger came to life, and with a whirl, he flung an off-balance Dan into the car and slammed the door. The suspicious umbrella Dan had been carrying clattered to the pavement, and Roger stared for a second as the fall caused ten inches of steel to suddenly extend from the umbrella's tip. He swooped down and scooped up the lethal umbrella, and then dashed back into the tavern, as he heard Dan shout, "Dammit, he's getting away!"

Inside the tavern door, Roger found a catch near the end of the umbrella. He touched it, and the ten inches of sharp steel slid back into the main shaft. He thought about calling the police or telling the bartender, but decided to just wait and see whether Dan followed him back into the tavern.

After waiting a couple of minutes, with no show by Dan, he tried calling his home again, to no avail. Then he dialed the number of his friend Kurt Strong.

Kurt had just walked into his apartment when the phone rang. It had been a busy day, and he groaned, "Oh, no!" but he obeyed the phone's insistent appeal. Kurt was used to calls at all hours due to the nature of his work. Clients needing investigative service frequently required it during hours other than nine to five. After he said, "Hello," he was inundated with a flood of agitated words from Roger about "being followed, drugged, kidnapped, slender dark man, black car, umbrella dagger, wife not answering phone . . ." A minute later, Kurt was in his car on his way to the Town Tavern, wondering what was going on.

It took Kurt less than fifteen minutes to get there. He found Roger sitting in a booth, watching the door. On the table were two drinks and a long, black umbrella.

"Thanks for coming, Kurt. I have a drink here for you." Roger seemed more composed now.

"Sounds like you've been having a bit of excitement," commented Kurt with a smile.

"Watch this," Roger said as he touched the release on the umbrella. The steel blade sprang into view.

Chapter 5

After filling Kurt in on what had happened, Roger asked, "What do you suggest I do now?"

"We could go to the police, but without evidence, except this umbrella, I'm not sure what they could do. Did you get the license number of the car?"

"No, I'm afraid not," admitted Roger. "Maybe I should get home, if you'll take me. Frankly, I'm a bit worried about Pat. She should have been home by now. You don't suppose—?" His voice trailed off; he hated to express the fear he was feeling.

"Now don't go imagining things. I'm sure Pat's okay," assured Kurt. "Come on; I'll give you a lift."

Outside, they looked about in the developing dusk of evening to see whether the big black car or the men were still there, but they saw nothing to alarm them. They did not notice the car parked in a driveway a block away, where they were being observed through a pair of binoculars.

On the way home, Roger speculated, "Do you think this has anything to do with my problem at work? You know, the Q-23 formula I told you about."

"I was wondering the same thing," admitted Kurt. But surely, your company isn't crazy enough to try to abduct you like this. What would be the purpose?"

"I don't know," mused Roger, "but that Soly is an odd duck. I wouldn't put anything past him."

Kurt's trained eyes spotted in his rearview mirror a pair of headlights trailing way behind them. He didn't want to alarm Roger further, and he wasn't sure whether was a tail or just a coincidence. Roger lived in a rather secluded area, with many trees extending into a forest preserve. His closest neighbor lived about half a block away. It was an ideal area to raise a family, but not so ideal from a security standpoint. Kurt became more convinced that they were being followed when he stopped in front of Roger's house. The following lights paused, then went out; in the dim glow of a streetlight, he could see a dark car pull over to the side of the road and stop.

Roger was out of the car like a shot, and called back, "The car is in the driveway. Pat must be home. Come in, Kurt. Come in with me."

Kurt followed after noting through the deepening darkness that no one got out of the car parked nearby. When he reached the house, Pat was explaining how she had been detained picking up their two children at their music lessons, so had not been home when Roger called. She had driven by the train station on the way home, probably just missing Roger when he was in the Town

Tavern. Roger looked relieved and a bit sheepish as he explained to Pat why Kurt was there, without really telling her the full story. He didn't want to scare Pat and the two children.

After a few minutes, and declining an invitation to stay to dinner, Kurt left. Before driving off, he noted that the dark car was still there. Kurt drove around the block, but he parked before reaching Roger's street, and then walked to the corner just in time to see the dark car, still with no lights, glide to the front of Roger's house.

Keeping out of the glow from a streetlight, staying in the sheltering darkness of trees, Kurt crept up behind the parked car. The front window on the passenger side of the car was rolled down. The two men in the car were talking softly as they gazed intently at the front of Roger's house. In the quiet of the evening, Kurt could hear snatches of conversation.

". . . to the door. Then get the hell out of the way."

Another gruff voice, "What if the wife or the damn kids come to the door?"

"Naw, not at night . . . the old man . . . this rifle."

Kurt cursed himself mentally for not bringing his revolver, but he preferred not to carry the gun except when he knew it might be needed. When Roger had called, he hadn't thought . . . But wait, there *was* a weapon back in his car. Again staying in the shadows, he ran back around the corner, and then scooped up the long, black umbrella from the backseat. As he started to retrace his path back to the rear of the car in front of Roger's house, he heard a car door close quietly, and in the dim light he saw a figure slink from the car up to the front porch of Roger's house.

Kurt found the umbrella's release button and watched the gleaming steel slide out. He reached the rear of the car as the man at the door of Roger's house rang the doorbell. Then like a big kid ringing doorbells at Hallowe'en, the man darted behind a clump of bushes beside the porch. As Kurt crept up the passenger side of the car, he saw a steel rifle barrel slowly extended out of the window. Then a man's left arm holding the middle of the rifle barrel rested on the door frame.

The porch light went on at Roger's house in response to the doorbell, and then Roger's tall form appeared at the door. Roger, seeing no one, opened the screen door and partially stepped out into the light, trying to peer into the darkness at the vague shape of a car he could see at the curb.

At this moment, Kurt lunged forward and penetrated the protruding left arm with ten inches of steel, as the night exploded with a rifle shot. The force of Kurt's charge forced the arm forward, back into the car, and skewered it to the padded dashboard. A scream of pain came from the car, and the umbrella was wrenched from Kurt's hand.

The man behind the bushes came out and ran to the car as Kurt ducked back behind it. As the man reached the car, he yelled, "What happened? You missed him. What the hell is going on?"

Between groans of pain and cursing, Kurt could make out ". . . stabbed by my own umbrella . . . see a damn thing . . . bleeding like a stuck pig . . . need a doctor." The two men took off in the car with a squeal of tires, never noticing Kurt crouched behind the car.

Roger had scrambled back into the house, slammed the door, and turned off the porch light. When he heard the car drive off, he cautiously opened the door. Kurt hailed him with, "Hey, Roger, you okay?"

"I guess so. What happened? I thought you left, Kurt."

"I did, but I came back," and he described what had happened. "Looks like I really owe you one, Kurt," admitted a grateful Roger. "Say, here come the police. Pat called them when she heard the shot. What should we tell them, Kurt?"

"Just tell them the facts," advised Kurt. "That is, what actually happened, nothing about our suspicions about your employer. That's not fact . . . yet."

As it turned out, the police did not seem fully convinced by their story, and on second thought, Kurt understood why. There was no actual evidence. The umbrella was gone, they couldn't find any bullet hole, and they had no witnesses. However, the police agreed to patrol the area all night, and also agreed to check out the car license number that Kurt had memorized.

After the police left, Kurt and Roger talked a while. Kurt asked, "Can Pat and the kids go somewhere for a few days?"

"I guess so. Pat's been wanting to go visit her mother in Michigan. I sure would like to get them away from this, whatever is going on."

"I doubt if these characters will be back tonight, especially the one I speared with that ten-inch blade. So I suggest you send your family off in the morning. Then give me a call, and we'll decide what to do next."

Chapter 6

LATER THAT SAME night, Sylvester Claybourne was alone in his bachelor apartment where he had lived for several years. He was standing in the living room in his maroon-colored bathrobe and matching slippers, staring out of the large picture window, which had a sweeping overview of scenic Lake Michigan. Lights from passing ships twinkled on the distant horizon, but Sylvester's eyes were not registering any of this panoramic view.

Brows furrowed, his face had a worried look. The phone call he had been anticipating should have come an hour ago. His third Scotch on the rocks was in his hand, which was one drink more than he usually allowed himself. Nervously he sat the glass down to reach into the side pocket of his bathrobe and pass a comb through his ever-groomed hair.

Again picking up his drink and returning to stare out of the window facing the lake, he sipped absentmindedly as he rocked from his toes to his heels and back again. When Sylvester Claybourne was alone, he did not always maintain the control that he prided himself on in public, especially at his job with Benson & Co. Under stress, he became moody and talked to himself. Downing the remains of his drink, he stalked to the built-in bar and muttered, "Damn him."

Sylvester was thinking of both Roger Pate and the man Roger knew as Dan Grover, whose real name was Dirk Gatsman. "Damn both of them," he said aloud. Then adding Benson Jr. to his thinking, "Damn all three of them." This made him feel a little better, as he stopped in front of a mirror to pass a comb through his hair, and then mixed his fourth drink.

After midnight, when the phone finally rang, he muttered to himself, "It's about time!" but when he picked up the phone, his voice was controlled. "Hello."

"This is Dirk."

"How did it go?"

"Not good; in fact, bad."

"Wasn't the job done?"

"No."

"Why not?"

"We made two attempts, and struck out both times. I ended up with my left arm slashed all to hell. My doctor said—"

"Look, I don't want any details about your problems. You were supposed to do a job, and it sounds like you botched it. It's imperative that the job be done properly before he talks to anyone. Now get back out there and complete the job."

"Don't talk to me that way, or you can get yourself another guy. There are two of them now, and the second guy is the one that got me in the arm."

"Who the hell is the second guy?"

"How the hell am I supposed to know?"

"Well, you'll have to get both of them; he probably knows the whole story now."

"That's fine with me. I don't like guys who stick a blade in me, but it doubles the price."

"Okay, okay. Just get it done quickly."

"It's a deal, but I've had more than enough of it for to-night. It's now Saturday morning. I'm going to get some sleep."

Sylvester paused, "On second thought, we have to find out whether anyone else knows what this is about. Before you finish them off, I need to talk to them. So just hold them somewhere, soften 'em up a bit, and get back to me before you complete the job."

"Hey," protested Dirk. "This is getting too complicated. You didn't say anything about—"

"Now listen," interrupted Soly, "I'm paying you plenty. We have to do it my way, or it's all off."

"Well, okay. Just so I get the guy that stuck me with that blade," agreed Dirk.

"Call me when you have them," advised Soly, "and make it soon."

CHAPTER 7

SATURDAY DAWNED bright and sunny, after Roger and Pat had spent a restless night. Pat could not talk Roger into leaving with her and the kids, so she busied herself early, getting breakfast and packing a few belongings. They were on their way by 9:00 a.m.

Roger phoned Kurt at his apartment. Kurt had already learned from the police that the license number he had given them was from a car reported stolen. Dead end there.

Kurt drove to Roger's house, and then joined Roger in having a cup of coffee as they discussed what to do.

"You should figure they will come back, even though they may not," warned Kurt.

"In other words, play it safe," agreed Roger. "I'll buy that, but what do I do to prepare?"

"For one thing—since this is the weekend—I'll stick around, if you want," offered Kurt.

"Well, you can be sure I want you to stick around," said Roger, with a smile.

"Okay," said Kurt. "Next you should call the police and ask them to patrol. Did they patrol last night?"

"Sure did. But early this morning they told me they couldn't keep it up after daylight, too many other special duties on Saturday."

"Oh, great," groaned Kurt. "Well, we'll have to get along without them. Let's check that your doors and windows are locked, and then just wait to see if anything happens."

Kurt and Roger spent the rest of the day in the house, keeping an eye on the street and grounds. They joked about the state of siege, and, since nothing developed, felt a little foolish; but remembering what had happened the previous day, they stuck to their watch. It gave them a chance to talk more than they usually did after their tennis games.

Late in the day, they discussed whether to stay at the house or go to Kurt's' apartment for the night.

"It would be safer at my apartment," said Kurt, "because there are fewer points of entry to watch."

Roger responded, "That would be safer than here, probably, but it wouldn't resolve anything. I'd like to bring this to a head. If anything is going to happen, let's have it happen—while my family is away."

"You make a good point," admitted Kurt. "Okay, we stay here, as long as the food and beer last. Say, maybe one of us should get some sleep now; it could be a long night."

"I'm not a bit sleepy," said Roger. "If you can sleep now, you're a better man than I."

"Well, I'll give it a try." Kurt stretched out on the sofa in the living room, and amazed Roger by falling asleep in a few minutes. Roger studied Kurt's relaxed, but strong features, and silently thanked Kurt for being with him. In spite of the unknown dangers they faced, Roger felt greatly relieved and confident with his friend present.

Chapter 8

Darkness fell outside, and Roger was careful to turn out the lights in each room. During one of the half-hourly tours they had agreed to maintain, he was looking out of the big bay window in the living room when some movement caught his attention. Not sure what it was, he knelt by the window and moved up close to the pane. The only light in the room was from a dim night lamp, which caused some glare in the window, and he shaded his eyes with one hand.

Suddenly a face came up from below the window, followed by a metal garbage can lid, which slammed into the big picture window with a crash that sent Roger falling backward in a shower of glass. This was closely followed by two men leaping through the broken window into the room. Each had a revolver in his hand.

Kurt sprang off the nearby sofa, but before he could reach for his gun, one of the men snarled, "Hold it, buster, and put your hands up." Kurt surveyed the scene in a glance, and then slowly raised his hands above his head. Roger was still on the floor, trying to staunch the blood flowing from a cut on his forehead.

"All right now, both of you get on the sofa."

They complied, although Roger seemed a bit dazed. In the dim light, Roger finally recognized one of the men. "You're the guy in the bar—Dan something. What the hell do you want?"

Dan, ignoring Roger, turned to his partner and said, "Take a look outside and see if anyone heard anything." After an "Everything looks quiet" report, the two intruders bound Kurt's and Roger's hands with drapery cord. The flow of blood from Roger's cut forehead had subsided, but his face and shirt were a scarlet mess.

"Keep a close eye on them," warned Dan, as he went into the kitchen and dialed a phone number.

"Okay, you can come talk to these two birds now. We got both of them trussed up in his living room, no problem. Just come to the front door."

During the next half hour, Dan and his cohort took turns raiding the refrigerator and watching their captives.

Kurt was working on his bound wrists behind his back. In his special training to obtain his private investigator's license, he had learned the trick of tensing his wrists when they were being tied to allow for some slack in the bonds. Now he was flexing his arms, putting tension on the cords to loosen their grip.

When the visitor arrived, he made no pretense at concealment as he confronted Roger with a half smile, saying, "You don't look very good, Roger."

"Soly!" exclaimed Roger. "What the devil are you doing? You can't get away with this."

"Roger, I tried to reason with you at the office, but you wouldn't be reasonable, so you brought this on yourself. Now I want to know just one thing. How far has this gone? Who besides this guy with you and your wife knows about Q-23?"

"She doesn't know anything, you louse. I'll admit that I told Kurt here, but that's all. And I wouldn't have told Kurt if you had agreed with my request."

Soly stared long at Roger. Then he seemed to make up his mind, and snapped, "You know what? I believe you are just dumb enough to be telling the truth." He turned to his two henchmen and said flatly, "Wait till I'm gone, and then take care of both of them. Make it look like a robbery."

Kurt had said nothing, but he had been thinking furiously. Now he announced, "There's one thing you should know."

Soly hesitated, "Yeah? What's that?"

"Before coming here, I took a precaution, in case something like this happened. I dictated a memo into my office machine, telling the whole story—including your name, Soly. Monday morning, my assistant will start investigating."

"You're a liar," snarled Sylvester.

"He may be," agreed Dan, "but maybe we should check it out."

"Don't be a sucker. He's just grasping at straws. Just wait about an hour, then do your job."

Soon after Sylvester Claybourne left, Kurt's work on his bonds was fruitful, but he kept his hands concealed behind his back. After what seemed like an eon, Kurt saw his opportunity. Dan was back in the kitchen, looking for another beer, and his helper was dozing in a chair, confident that their victims were tied securely. With a gracefully coordinated move of his athletic body, Kurt scooped up a heavy ceramic figurine from the table near the sofa, and then crashed it down on his captor's head. This really put him the guy to sleep, as he slumped from the chair onto the floor.

Roger struggled to his feet as Kurt grabbed his arm and propelled them out the front door, just before Dan burst into the room with gun drawn. He fired one futile shot out the open door into the darkness, and then bent to arouse his fallen comrade.

Outside the house, Kurt and Roger raced around the side and into the forbidding, but sheltering woods. They were followed a minute later by their former captors, with drawn guns. The woods led to a forest preserve, and after Kurt released the cord around Roger's arms, Roger took the lead, as he was acquainted with these woods. Many were the times he had taken his family on walks among the pleasant, friendly trees. However, that had been in the daytime, and now the woods had an entirely different aspect and mood. In the darkness, every tree and bush was an obstacle, and the armed enemy behind them was a frantic presence forcing them onward. Roger and Kurt moved as silently as they could and spoke only in whispers, while their hunters, knowing they were unarmed, stumbled with confidence, making no pretence at being quiet.

Chapter 9

Roger finally led Kurt to a recreation area in the preserve, where they stopped to rest behind a supply shed. They could hear their pursuers crashing through the brush, cursing at the woods and at each other. Before long they heard, "We'll never find 'em in this god-forsaken jungle."

"Let's get the hell out of here."

Kurt and Roger waited till they could no longer hear their enemy retreating.

"Do you think it's safe to go back?" asked Roger.

"Not on your life—or mine, either," responded Kurt. "They may be waiting somewhere along the way or in the house, expecting us to wander back, and planning to pick us off."

"So what do we do?"

Kurt pondered a bit. "Is there a road around here somewhere?"

"Yes, Elm Road. It can't be more than half a mile; a bike path near here crosses it. Follow me."

After a few moments of stumbling around, they were on the bicycle path, and after about ten minutes, came to the road.

"There's a gas station down this way. I hope it's still open."

It wasn't, but there was an outdoor pay phone. They were able to get a taxi, and then Kurt insisted on taking Roger to the emergency room at the closest hospital. The cut on Roger's forehead took five stitches and a big white bandage. While the doctor was working on Roger, Kurt was telling their tale to the police. This time, the police seemed to take them seriously. From the hospital, they were driven in a squad car to Roger's house. The broken window and other damage to the house interested the police. They convinced Roger to stay home, with a policeman as guard. His head was starting to throb from his wound, so he did not object strenuously. Kurt accompanied the police to Sylvester Claybourne's apartment.

CHAPTER 10

THE BIG, ORNATE clock in the lobby of the South Lake Tower Plaza Apartments was gently chiming 11:00 p.m. when Kurt and two policemen entered. One of these was a lieutenant named Neal Brinkley, a tall, square-jawed veteran of fifteen years. The other was Corporal Tim Conrad, two years on the force. The lieutenant pushed the little plastic button next to Sylvester Claybourne's name. Through the speaker came a woman's voice, "Yes?"

"This is Lieutenant Neal Brinkley, with the police department. We would like to see Mr. Sylvester Claybourne."

"Oh dear, he was just going to bed. I'll check with him. Hold on." A minute later, "He said to come up."

The massive inner door buzzed insistently, until Corporal Conrad relieved its inner workings with a push. At the apartment on the tenth floor, the door was held open by a delicate-looking young woman clad in a frilly robe that only partly covered up a revealing nightgown. She ushered them into a large, well-furnished living room, where Sylvester Claybourne was standing with his back to the immense window that overlooked Lake Michigan. He was clad in an expensive-looking maroon bathrobe, which covered pajama pants that went down to his bedroom slippers. He advanced with a friendly smile, and said, "Well, what can I do for you gentlemen?" He showed no sign of recognition toward Kurt as he addressed himself to Lieutenant Brinkley.

The lieutenant responded formally with, "Mr. Claybourne, we are investigating a report that you are involved in certain violent acts that occurred at the home of your employee, Roger Pate, specifically, that you visited his home earlier this evening. What do you have to say about this?"

"That's crazy," retorted Claybourne. "I've been here all evening. With Dotty," he said, waving a hand toward the young lady who was now seated on the edge of a huge semicircular sofa that dominated the room.

"That's right," she volunteered. "We've both been here all evening. It's been very cozy. Don't you think this is a very romantic room, with the fireplace and the view of that great big lake out there?" She smiled and snuggled her pert head onto her exposed right shoulder.

Lieutenant Brinkley continued to question the two occupants for ten minutes or so, without shaking their story. Kurt muzzled his desire to enter into the questioning. He had been allowed to accompany the two officers after agreeing that he would not participate in the questioning. His only contribution was a positive response to the identification of Sylvester Claybourne as the person who visited Roger Pate's house.

On the way down in the elevator, Lieutenant Brinkley confessed to a frustrated Kurt that he was convinced, "They're both lying through their teeth," but explained that he felt it best to do some more investigating and obtain additional evidence before considering an arrest.

When they arrived back at Roger's house, Kurt found a police guard at the door and Roger sound asleep in his bed. Kurt drove to his apartment, mulling over what had happened and what he would do tomorrow—or actually today—as he noted it was now 1:30 a.m. Sunday morning.

CHAPTER 11

ON SUNDAY, Kurt and Roger spent several hours at the police station, giving their stories in detail and reviewing mug shots, trying to identify the two intruders, though without success.

Monday morning, Roger reported to work as usual, still wearing a bandage on his forehead. He and Kurt had discussed whether he should take some special action at work. Roger wanted to confront Soly. However, Kurt advised, and Roger finally agreed, to wait and see what developed.

At 9:15 a.m., Sylvester Claybourne's secretary, Betty, called Roger on the intercom. "Mr. Claybourne would like to see you."

"Well, if old Soly wants to see me, tell him to come to my little old laboratory," Roger retorted to a startled Betty. She was even more startled when her boss seemed to meekly accept the invitation.

Sylvester closed the door quietly after entering the laboratory. Then he came directly to the point. "Roger, I'm really sorry about what has happened."

"Sorry!" exploded Roger. "You should be put in jail! You—"

"Yes, I know," interrupted Soly, "but hear me out. What I did was wrong, I admit, but I'll make it up to you if you'll give me a chance. What I have in mind is compensating you for the trouble I've caused. I'll pay you twenty-five thousand dollars if you'll forget what has happened and forget Q-23." He was almost begging, as his voice took on a whining tone and his face twisted up, while the ever-present comb was passed through his well-combed hair.

"Are you crazy?" Roger asked. "Don't you realize what you have done can't be bought off with money? The police are involved now. They are going to investigate you, and you are going to land in jail where you belong."

"Not if you don't push it; it'll die off. Nothing bad has actually happened. I'll pay for the damage to your house. Look, take the money, please," he pleaded. "I'll feel better, and you'll be better off; you can use the money, can't you?"

Roger paused for a minute as he thought. Then he replied, "Of course, I could use the money. In fact, I could use four times that amount."

"What!" shouted Soly. "You mean one hundred thousand dollars?"

"That's right, one hundred thousand dollars—and I'll take care of the damage to my house myself."

Soly's face flushed as anger welled up in him, but he gulped and controlled himself. "All right, damn it! It's a hundred thousand dollars. I'll have part of it ready in five days." Then he wheeled around and stalked out the door.

CHAPTER 12

THAT NIGHT, ROGER and Kurt met at the Side Door Bar and Grill, and Roger described the confrontation with Soly. Kurt had a puzzled look on his face. "Do you actually mean you are considering taking the money and dropping the charges?"

"Well," Roger spoke slowly, "I haven't decided. That's why I'm talking to you. I need to think this out, and I need your advice. There are many things to consider here."

"Like what things?" asked Kurt.

"Okay, I made a list. Maybe it's my scientific training," grinned Roger, as he pulled out a crumpled piece of paper from his pocket and read:

Considerations for Taking the Money
1. I could use the money.
2. It would really hurt Soly financially. In fact, it might hurt him more than a criminal sentence, if he gets one.

3. It would call off Soly from making any further attacks against me and my family.

Considerations against Taking the Money

1. It is not legal or morally right.
2. Soly would not go to jail like he should.
3. Acceptance would mean bottling up Q-23.

Kurt's first thought was, no way should Roger consider taking the money. However, perhaps there was a way that this latest development could be used for Roger's benefit. He mused aloud, "It could be tricky, and maybe dangerous, but it's worth considering."

"What are you saying?" queried Roger.

"Well, Roger, I'm not recommending that you accept Soly's offer, based on normal considerations. I agree with you that it's on the edge of being improper or illegal. However, you are not dealing with a normal situation, or with a person who is morally or ethically normal. Soly has proven that he is capable of murder. But with his girlfriend, Dolly, backing up his story, it's just their word against ours. We need some more concrete evidence."

Chapter 13

THE NEXT few days passed routinely. Roger had his house repaired, and his family returned. On the fifth day after his meeting with Soly, Roger was prepared. In his desk in the laboratory office was a tape recorder.

Soly came into the lab office, shut the door carefully, and sat down across the desk from Roger. Roger had pushed the tape recorder button as soon as he saw Soly coming into the laboratory, and then settled back into his chair.

A solemn-faced, controlled-voice Soly began with, "Roger, I have twenty-five thousand dollars ready for you; the rest will take a bit longer."

"Soly," said a composed Roger. "Let's talk a bit about how this is going to work. First, let's confirm what you are going to do, and then what you expect of me."

"Okay," agreed Soly, with a smile that was more a grimace, "But don't expect me to put it in writing. I'm going to give you one hundred thousand dollars—the first twenty-five thousand dollars now, and the remaining seventy-five thousand dollars as soon as I can."

"That 'as soon as I can' is not good enough," Roger stated flatly. "I'll give you one week to pay in full."

Sylvester squirmed in his chair, and his voice lost its control, as he pleaded, "But I'll lose everything! I'll have to sell all my stock in Benson and sell my car. How about if I—"

"No," butted in Roger. "It's one week, or it's no deal."

"All right, all right," conceded a shaken Sylvester, as he got up from his chair and paced nervously, pausing only to pull out his comb and pass it through his hair. "Now for your part! You agree to forget about Q-23, and to forget about the recent unfortunate incident at your home, and agree not to—"

"Unfortunate incident!" scoffed Roger. "You mean attempted murder of me and my friend, Kurt Strong!"

"I'm sorry about that, Roger, but I was under a lot of pressure; I wouldn't have tried it if you had been reasonable about the Q-23. Anyway, are we agreed now?"

"Sure, why not?" said a smiling Roger. "Where's the twenty-five thousand dollars?"

Sylvester pulled out his wallet from his coat pocket and removed a cashier's check, which he handed to Roger, who said, "Cashier's check for twenty-five thousand dollars, made out to Roger Pate, dated today, May 23, signed by Sylvester Claybourne."

"Hey, what's going on?" cried a suddenly suspicious Sylvester. "Why are you reading off that check? Sounds like you've been taping this."

"You're right," admitted Roger. "It's all on tape now." Roger rose from his chair, walked to the door, opened it, and said, "Thank you very much for your confession, Soly, to attempted murder and bribery. The tape will be turned over to the police."

Sylvester's look of consternation quickly turned to rage, and he rushed to Roger's desk, pulling out drawers, trying to find the tape recorder. However, he was no match for the taller, athletic Roger, who merely enclosed a squirming Sylvester in a bear hug, lifted him bodily from the floor, and deposited him outside the office. Sylvester glared at him and spat out, "You haven't heard the last of this!" and then stalked off.

CHAPTER 14

ROGER SAT MUSING in his office after Soly had left. For the first time, he felt rather secure and in charge of the situation. He could keep the twenty-five thousand dollars—and probably still obtain the additional seventy-five thousand dollars—or he could do as he had told Soly, and turn the tape over to the police. His contemplations soon led him to the realization that actually he had only one choice, which was to turn the tape over to the police. With a sigh and a half smile, he muttered to himself, "But it would have been nice to spend that hundred thousand dollars," as he dialed his phone.

"Is Kurt Strong in?" asked Roger.

"No, he's out for at least another hour. This is his assistant, Ray Grayson. Can I help you?"

"I'd like to leave a message. Ask Kurt to give me a call as soon as possible. This is Roger Pate; he has my number."

"Okay, I'll give him the message as soon as he comes in," responded Ray.

Roger busied himself around the lab, waiting for Kurt to call, but he would not have been so complacent if he had known what Sylvester Claybourne was up to in another part of the building.

After leaving Roger's office, Sylvester stormed back to his office, brushing by his secretary, Betty, who tried to give him a message, and slammed the door in her face. Sylvester felt trapped like a rat, and, like a trapped rat, he was dangerous and determined to strike back. Shortly after he had returned to his office, Betty noticed from the light on her telephone that Mr. Claybourne was on the phone.

CHAPTER 15

IT WAS LATE in the afternoon before Kurt called Roger back with, "What's up, Roger?" Roger tried to sound nonchalant, but his voice had a note of triumph as he reported, "I've got it on tape. Soly, admitting to attempted murder and bribery, also his check for twenty-five thousand dollars."

"Great; sounds like it went as we planned," said Kurt.

"Just like a script," Roger enthused. "Except at the end, he got suspicious, and I admitted it was all on tape. He got a bit belligerent, but I was able to take care of it. He buzzed out, mad as a bumblebee."

"That doesn't sound good," cautioned Kurt. "Knowing what Soly is capable of doing, we'd better get that tape to Lieutenant Brinkley as soon as possible."

"I suppose you're right," admitted Roger.

"Tell you what," said Kurt. I'll phone Lieutenant Brinkley and then meet you at the police station. I'll meet you there in half an hour."

Roger had just put the tape and the check in his coat pocket, and was ready to leave the office, when in walked Sylvester with a sardonic grin on his face. Sylvester closed the door behind him and said tauntingly, "Okay, wise guy. Two can play at this game, and I can get dirtier than you."

"Oh," responded Roger. "Just what do you plan on doing?"

"It's not what I plan to do; it's what I've already done—to your wife and kids," said Sylvester, as he settled himself in a chair and stared smugly at Roger.

Roger felt a cold chill go up his spine, as he became aware of the depth of degeneracy that this man was capable of, and he inwardly cursed himself for not realizing this earlier.

"What have you done to my family?" Roger asked with dry lips.

"Well, not much yet," gloated Sylvester. "But just say they are in my custody, and nothing will happen to them if you cooperate. If you don't cooperate—I'll leave that to your imagination."

"You're lying!" yelled Roger. "You're just trying to scare me into giving you that tape."

"I agree I'm trying to scare you," admitted Sylvester. "But I'm not lying about your family. Right now they are being held at your house by those two associates of mine, whom you have previously met."

"I still don't believe you," said Roger. He picked up his phone and started to dial. With a twisted smile, Sylvester crooned, "Your home phone is dead, and I advise you to cooperate, or that won't be the only thing dead at your house."

Roger listened to the busy signal buzz repeatedly in his ear, and then he slowly replaced the phone in its cradle.

CHAPTER 16

SYLVESTER PULLED out of the parking garage, with Roger sitting beside him in the front seat. They both were quiet until Sylvester pulled off the main highway to take the side roads to Roger's house. Sylvester glanced over at Roger and announced, "Well, it's about that time, Roger."

"What do you mean?" asked Roger.

"It's time for you to hand over the tape and that twenty-five thousand dollar check," responded Sylvester.

"Not on your life," growled Roger. "Not until I see that my wife and kids are okay. And if you try anything now, I'll beat you to a—" Roger's words faded away as he felt a cold metal ring of steel pressed against the back of his neck. A wicked snicker came from the back seat, and turning around, Roger found the threatening face and gun of the man with the umbrella.

"That's right, Roger," gleefully exulted Sylvester, as he pulled the car over to the side of the nearly deserted road. "He's been on the back floor under a blanket. Now hand over that tape and my check if you want to live to see your family again. And don't worry about your family; we never even approached them. I'm not stupid enough to put my head in a noose by kidnapping your precious family. All we did was cut the phone wire to your house." He chortled, and then his face became stern as he spat out, "Hand it over!"

Glumly, though relieved about his family, Roger took out the tape and check, and gave them to Sylvester, who then ordered, "Now get out of the car. By the way, you're fired. I hired you, and I am now firing you. Don't bother to come into the office. We will be sending you your personal items from the office and your last paycheck."

Roger stood by the side of the road, watching the car with the two men take off into the distance. He felt totally defeated, and, with sagging shoulders, he started trudging toward his house, which was still about a mile away.

Kurt was sitting in Lieutenant Brinkley's office, glancing at his wristwatch. "I don't understand what's keeping him, Lieutenant. It's been at least an hour since I talked to Roger, and he should have been here before now."

The phone on the officer's desk rang. "This is Lieutenant Brinkley." He listened briefly and then said, "Hold on." Turning to Kurt, he said, "Here is your friend, Roger Pate," and handed the receiver to Kurt.

After asking, "What happened?" Kurt listened intently for some time to Roger's report. "So we are back to where we were, with no concrete evidence, but at least you and your family are okay. I'll explain what happened to Lieutenant Brinkley, and I'll be over this evening after dinner where we can talk further."

Chapter 17

Roger and Kurt were sitting in the den of Roger's house. It was a small room, dominated by a large wooden desk and two rambling bookcases, one filled with technical books and the other with a variety of fiction, including some serious classics. While overcrowded, it was Roger's favorite room, where he could get away to work, think, and read. He was seated at the desk, while Kurt was in the room's only other chair, which was large and comfortable with a floor lamp, where Roger had spent many hours reading.

"Boy, did I ever louse up," moaned Roger. "Everything was looking great until—"

"There's no sense crying over spilt milk," said Kurt. "Let's look at where we are and what we can do next."

"You're right," Roger agreed, and after a moment of silence, "I suppose I could still go back to the office and tell my story to Mr. Benson Jr., or even Benson Sr., but why would they believe me over Soly?"

"I'm afraid you're in a bit of a hole, Roger," said Kurt. And the two of them sat silently, thinking. In the distant background they could hear the TV in the living room, bleating out its message to Roger's family.

Kurt began musing out loud. "Benson & Co. has treated you rather shabbily, to put it mildly. Or at least your boss at Benson has. You are out of a job, and basically, it's because you've done a good job. But one thing you do have is that formula for Q-23; you did tell me you removed all Q-23 papers from the lab, didn't you?"

"That's right. It's all right here in the bottom drawer," Roger said, as he patted the side of the desk.

"So why don't you develop Q-23 yourself now?" asked Kurt. "In my opinion, Benson & Co. has given up any moral right to Q-23 because of the way they have treated you, plus they have not only not developed it, they have tried to squelch it. As for any legal rights to Q-23, I doubt they would want to publicly fight for it. The way they have handled this whole thing would result in too much bad publicity for Benson & Co."

Roger's dejected attitude had faded slowly as he listened to Kurt, and he now chimed in with, "This may turn out to have been a blessing in disguise. I'm sure Q-23 has tremendous potential. The only thing is, I'm not sure I could handle all the aspects myself. Say, how about us becoming partners in the development of Q-23?"

Kurt stared at Roger for a long moment, and then extended his hand with a smile, as he said, "Shake, partner."

Chapter 18

DURING THE NEXT few months, Roger and Kurt developed their partnership. Roger worked on the project full time and invested twenty thousand dollars, while Kurt spent half his time with Roger and invested forty thousand dollars. They found and rented a small, empty warehouse located on the edge of town, purchased some equipment, and bought the raw materials needed to produce their first batch of Q-23, which they now named Hair-Ban.

Their primary expenditure was for a large batch kettle in which to mix and heat the ingredients for Hair-Ban. The kettle, made of gleaming stainless steel, was ten feet in diameter, and, standing on its support, it was ten feet in height. The kettle was Roger's pride and joy, and he carefully cleaned it before even thinking about adding the first materials for the first batch of Hair-Ban. "There must be no contamination," he told Kurt. Roger's duties were producing and bottling Hair-Ban.

However, before making up a commercial batch, Kurt and Roger decided they needed to make a laboratory sample, to reconfirm the product's effectiveness and to further test any complications that might arise from overdose or use on sensitive skin areas.

Kurt's legal training and insurance claims experience rose to the surface as he commented to Roger, "We wouldn't be able to buy enough liability insurance if thousands of customers developed skin problems from this product."

Roger set up a small laboratory in a corner of their building, and after a few days, he had reproduced a small quantity of the Q-23 he had made for Benson & Co. Roger held up two small bottles filled with the light green liquid. "Well, Kurt, here are our first bottles of Q-23. The only difference is that I added a little green food coloring."

"Wrong," corrected Kurt. "It's our first bottles of Hair-Ban."

"You are right," agreed Roger, as he waggled one of the bottles. In the glow of the overhead lights, he watched the dancing bubbles gently float around like the snowflakes in a paperweight he had had as a child. "Sure is pretty."

"Okay, back to earth, Roger," smiled Kurt. "I'll be the guinea pig this time. I assume your face is still stubble-free."

"Yep," said Roger, running his hand over his chin and cheeks. "Greatest thing since sliced bread. All right, you try it on your face, and I'll try it on some other parts of my body. I've often had the feeling that my wife, Pat, would prefer that I didn't have any hair on my chest, so I'll try it out there and under my arms too."

"Don't go too far," grinned Kurt, "or she may think she's sleeping with the wrong guy."

"Yeah," agreed Roger. "She might get too much of a kick out of that."

The next morning, Kurt shaved the left half of his face with his electric razor, and applied Hair-Ban to the other half with the cotton-tip applicator Roger had attached to the screw-type bottle of Hair-Ban. The lotion felt cool and soft on his face, with a slight, but not unpleasant, tingling sensation. Watching himself in the mirror, the short hair bristles on his face seemed to wilt and then vanish. Within three minutes of application, the right side of his face was entirely free of any sign of hair.

"Wow," he muttered to himself in the mirror. "This stuff really works."

Like a kid with a new toy, he next swabbed an area on the bottom part of his left leg, just above the ankle, where the hairs were one-half to one inch long. Again, as he watched in fascination, the hairs seemed to wilt, and within three minutes were entirely gone.

That same morning, Roger took out his bottle of Hair-Ban, and, holding it up, announced, "Pat, here is the product. How about witnessing me trying it out on various parts of my body."

Pat looked up with concern on her face. "Oh, Roger, are you sure it's safe?"

"Sure, it's okay. Remember, I used it on my face a long time ago and had no problem, except my razor has been gathering dust ever since."

"Well, you don't expect me to dust in your medicine cabinet, do you?" joked Pat.

"No, just kidding about the dust," Roger assured her. "I am now going to put some of this Hair-Ban under one armpit. Do you want to watch?"

"It sounds rather gross to me," said Pat making a face, "but I'll watch."

"Here goes," announced Roger, as he held his left arm high and swabbed his underarm with the applicator. Pat peered intently under his arm, and in less than a minute, reported, "Your hair is looking real sick."

"What do you mean, sick?" asked Roger.

"Well, it just looks sick, and getting sicker all the time; in fact, it looks dead now. The poor little hairs, they're all gone," she said.

"That was the idea," concurred Roger. "Hair in certain parts of the body no longer serves any purpose. In fact, it's a nuisance to most people. Next, I'm going to try this Hair-Ban on the hair on my chest."

"What!" exclaimed Pat. "Don't you dare. I love your chest the way it is," she said as she ran her fingers through the hairs on his chest.

"Not even in the interest of science?" asked Roger.

"Not even in the interest of science," Pat stated flatly. "But I'll tell you what. In the interest of science, I'll try it on me in a few places. After all, you need to know if it works on women too. I'll try it on my legs."

"Well, if you want to," agreed Roger. "But only a small area at first, till we see whether there is any problem, like an irritation or rash, or something."

"How does your armpit feel?" asked Pat.

"It feels fine," said Roger, rubbing it with his hand, "except it feels funny without any hair."

Late that day at the plant, Roger was looking intently at Kurt's face and Roger started to smile. "Your five o'clock shadow is at half-mast, Kurt."

"What do you mean?" asked Kurt, rubbing his face with his hand. "Oh, yeah, my stubble is back on the left side, but not on the right side. I hereby announce that Hair-Ban really works!"

Chapter 19

KURT DEVOTED his efforts to the business end of their project, including developing sales contacts, distribution, and publicity. Having no knowledge about the marketing of such a product, Kurt was at a loss regarding how to proceed. With their limited financial resources, an expensive advertising campaign was not practical. Also, he had no contacts with wholesale or retail marketing organizations, and no real desire to start trying to make such contacts.

"This is such a tremendous product," enthused Kurt to Roger. "It should sell itself."

"Like the old saying," commented Roger. "If you build a better mousetrap, the public will beat a path to your door."

"Well, this is a better mousetrap," Kurt declared, "but we still need to let folks know about it so they can beat a path to our door. You know, Roger, if we could get some newspaper to write an article about this new product, maybe it would give us some inexpensive publicity."

"Sounds like a good idea," agreed Roger.

The next morning, Kurt walked into the editorial office of the *Tribune* and asked to see the editor.

"What is the purpose of your visit?" politely asked the attractive young receptionist, with a bright smile for the handsome man standing before her.

"I have a story I think would be of interest," responded Kurt with a broad smile, and eyes that sparkled with interest.

"I'm sure it would," she murmured under her breath, and then catching herself, "What sort of story are you talking about?"

"Well, it's actually about a new type of cosmetic," stated Kurt.

"Oh, I'm afraid our editor normally isn't interested in anything like that," admitted the receptionist regretfully. "However, perhaps one of our assistant editors might talk to you. Do you have a calling card?"

Kurt produced a card, and, after looking at the card and checking her switchboard, she said, "Mr. Strong, the only assistant editor who's available now is Mr. Echen. I'll ring him for you."

A minute later, Kurt entered the cluttered, glassed-in cubbyhole office of Assistant Editor Howard Echen, who was about the same age as Kurt. But there the similarity ended. Howard Echen was a small, but husky, bearded man, with a nervous manner. He was fiddling with a pencil as he looked critically at Kurt's card. "Mr.

Kurt Strong, from Strong Consulting and Investigating Service. Well, what can I do for you?"

"It's about a new cosmetic product that I think would be of interest to your readers," stated Kurt. "It's a—"

"Hold on," interrupted Echen, tapping rapidly on his desk with his pencil. "We are not interested in providing free advertising for a new cosmetic. Now if you want to place an ad about your cosmetic, I'll send you to our advertising department."

"Well, it's not a regular cosmetic," explained Kurt. "You see, we have come up with an entirely new product, a new discovery. Actually, it's a new hair remover."

"A hair remover!" scoffed Echen. "That's nothing new. There are lots of hair removers on the market."

"Not like this one," insisted Kurt. "For instance, you could remove that beard from your face and never have to shave again."

"What's wrong with my beard?" the assistant editor asked defensively.

"No offense intended," soothed Kurt. "But if you ever wanted to be clean-shaven, you could do it without shaving with this new product."

"Well, I don't want to be clean-shaven," insisted Harold Echen. "Anyway, it still sounds like something more for our advertising department. Let me think about it and get back to you if we want to check further. I have your card."

On his way out, the receptionist asked Kurt, "How did it go with Mr. Echen?"

"I'm afraid that Mr. Echen was not very interested in my story," confessed Kurt. "In fact, he seemed a bit irritated with me."

"Don't take it personally," she confided. "He's like that sometimes." She obviously wanted to prolong the conversation with this attractive man. "You mentioned a new type of cosmetic. If it's for us ladies, I probably could use it."

Kurt smiled and then, cocking his head with an exaggerated look of appraisal, reported, "I don't see how you could possibly be improved upon." This compliment, plus Kurt's smile, gave rise to a warm glow of excitement in the young lady. Before she could recover herself to think of a follow-up comment, he was gone.

A short time later, Harold Echen came out of his office and said gruffly to the receptionist, "Sissy, you should know better than to bother me with a guy like that, promoting some dumb cosmetic."

"I'm sorry, Mr. Echen," Sissy confessed. "But he seemed so nice, and he said it was something new, like some new type of cosmetic.

"Ah, it's just some stupid hair remover," growled Echen, stroking his beard.

"Oh," exclaimed Sissy. "That sounds interesting." She hesitated, and then offered, "Mr. Echen, when I started here five months ago as receptionist, you said that you would give me a chance to develop a story sometime. How about giving me this one?"

"What?" exclaimed Echen. "There's no story here. You'd be wasting your time and ours."

"Well," offered Sissy, "how about if I only wasted my own time. I'll do it in my off-hours—no cost to the paper."

"Suit yourself," said Echen as he tossed Kurt's card onto her desk.

Sissy—whose real name was Doris Lang, but was nicknamed Sissy when her older brother had so called her instead of "sister"—was of average height, with a perky appearance and attitude. Two years out of college with a degree in communications, she had left a boring job with an advertising firm to try to make it as a writer in the newspaper field. However, the best offer she had had was this "temporary" position as receptionist.

Sissy studied Kurt's card. She was puzzled and intrigued by "Strong Consulting and Investigating Service." It sure didn't sound like a cosmetic firm. She smiled as she admitted to herself that Kurt Strong himself interested her.

Chapter 20

WHEN A SOMEWHAT dejected Kurt arrived back at his office later that morning, he was surprised when his assistant, Ray Grayson, greeted him with, "Sounds like you did pretty well at the *Tribune*."

"What do you mean?" asked Kurt. "The guy I saw isn't going to do anything for us."

"Well," responded Ray, "I don't know about any guy, but some sexy-sounding gal said she's from the *Tribune* and wants to meet you for lunch." He handed a telephone call slip to Kurt.

An hour later, Sissy and Kurt were sitting at a table in the Lake Street Grill. She listened intently and took notes on a pad as Kurt told her about Hair-Ban. The time seemed to fly by for both of them, until she glanced at her watch and said, "Oh dear, I have to get back to the office."

"Does that mean you're not interested?" asked Kurt.

"Not at all!" Sissy exclaimed. "I think this could be a great special interest story, but I'll need to see your plant and get more information. Tomorrow is Saturday. Could I meet you at your plant, say about nine in the morning?"

Sissy, Kurt, and Roger spent most of the next day together, going through the operation and demonstrating the product. During the tour of the plant, at one point where there were some obstacles on the floor, Kurt took Sissy's hand, and they were both aware of the flow of magnetism between them. Their hands remained together after the obstacle had been passed, until she gently squeezed his hand and then withdrew hers.

By midafternoon, Sissy had all the material she needed. Before she left, Kurt asked her with a smile, "Now that you know all about me and our operation, how about you filling me in on you at dinner tonight?"

"I really should work on this story tonight," she hesitated, "but that's too tempting an offer. The story will wait until tomorrow."

Later that evening, Sissy and Kurt were seated at the Café Bohemia, which was one of Kurt's favorite eating places. "As you can see from the menu," he explained, "they specialize in wild game dishes."

"I'm afraid I don't know anything about wild game," admitted Sissy, "but I'm sure I don't want any of the venison that's listed—those poor deer."

"I hope you're not a vegetarian," said Kurt with a smile, "because if you are, we're at the wrong place."

"No, I'm not a vegetarian," said Sissy, "but it does seem a shame that we have to eat animals."

"Well, until they invent a simulated steak that tastes as good as a real steak, I'm a dedicated meat eater."

With a little shrug of her shoulders and a smile, Sissy admitted, "I must confess I am too. Since you have been here before, how about you ordering for both of us, as long as it's not any of the venison!"

"Okay," Kurt agreed. "We will have one of their other specialties—roast duck."

Later, at the door to her apartment, Sissy turned to Kurt with, "I've had a wonderful time—being with you—and the roast duck was scrumptious, the best I've ever had."

Without a word, Kurt took her elbows in his hands, pulled her close, and slowly their lips met in a kiss they both felt long after they had parted.

The next Monday morning, Sissy handed in her story. Mr. Echen, the assistant editor, looked a bit skeptical when Sissy placed it on his desk. "You really wasted your own time on that dumb cosmetic?"

Sissy smiled her sweetest and said, "I really think it's a good story."

Grudgingly, Echen said, "Well, I'll look it over, and if it has any merit, I'll take it with me to the editorial meeting at 10:00 a.m. They are always looking for special items."

After Sissy had left, Mr. Echen quickly ran through the neatly typed story she had worked on all Sunday.

His skeptical look gradually turned to admiration for the way Sissy had presented the story and maintained his interest throughout. "Not bad," he muttered as he made only a couple of minor editorial changes.

The morning the article appeared in the paper, Mr. Benson Jr., of Benson & Co., stalked into Sylvester Claybourne's office and threw the paper on his desk. "Did you see this? What the hell is going on?" growled Mr. Benson Jr. "Is this that formula that Roger Pate developed for us?"

Sylvester quickly read the article, and then he felt his stomach turn over in a knot. Since he had fired Roger Pate, he thought his troubles were over. There had been no further talk about Q-23, he had heard nothing from Roger, he had hired a new chief chemist, and Mr. Benson Jr. had been talking about their need to make a decision on some management changes, including the post of executive vice president, which Sylvester was longing to fill. Now here was an irate Mr. Benson Jr. in his office, waiting for an answer. "Well, what about it, Sylvester?" insisted Mr. Benson Jr.

"Sounds like it might be," admitted Sylvester, hauling out his comb to run it through his crowning glory.

"You're damn right it sounds like it," fumed Mr. Benson Jr. "Now look here, Sylvester; you fired Roger Pate, and if the result of your actions is going to cost Benson & Co. some money, it's going to cost you too. You'd better do something about this, and do it quick. We are in a hell of a spot. We can't claim publicly 'This is our formula' without us looking bad."

Sylvester tried to calm Mr. Benson Jr. with, "Let me look into it further, Mr. Benson, and I'll get back to you."

"Okay," agreed Mr. Benson Jr., "but I don't want to just hear what you find out. I want you to take care of it. I don't care how; in fact, I don't want to know. I just don't want this product on the market; understand?"

"I'll take care of it," agreed Sylvester.

Chapter 21

It was two days later when Kurt visited their little warehouse factory to determine how the first batch was coming. He had to know when the first bottled product would be available so he could coordinate distribution for the test-marketing program he had developed. After he entered the warehouse, he watched Roger, who was busy on a ladder, taking a sample from the top of the large batch kettle.

Kurt yelled up to Roger, "Well, is the soup done?"

Roger almost dropped the sample as he looked down. "If I drop this sample on your lovely head of hair, we would find out pretty quick," laughed Roger as he slammed the lid on the kettle and climbed down. "No, it's not ready yet, but another couple of hours should do it. Then, tomorrow, we can start bottling the first batch of Hair-Ban."

Later that night, a car stopped a short distance from the warehouse. It was a dark night, but from the faint glow of a streetlight, two men could be seen in the car—Sylvester Claybourne and Dirk Gateman, alias Dan Grover.

"Are you sure that's the place?" asked Sylvester.

"Sure I'm sure," gruffly responded Dirk. "I cased the joint last night and even saw that Pate guy leave. It was just about this time. He must still be there. The lights are still on." They watched the warehouse until finally Sylvester nudged his dozing companion. "There he is," as Roger Pate came out the door, climbed into his car, and drove off, without noticing the parked car and its two occupants.

"Okay, here's what I want you to do," directed Sylvester, as he reached into the backseat and held up a five-gallon can. "Break in, spread this gas around, light it, and get back out here fast. I'll have the motor running, and we take off. It's as simple as that. Make sure you spread this stuff heavy around the area where he's been working, 'cause I want that to get it good."

"Yeah," retorted Dirk. "You probably want me to get it good, too. Then you wouldn't have to pay me off."

"What are you talking about, you lunkhead? I've already paid you plenty," responded Sylvester.

"Well, I don't like it," scowled Dirk. "I do all the dirty jobs and the dangerous work, while you sit back, fat and sassy."

"All right," conceded Sylvester. "Quit your bitching. I'll come in with you. I want to make sure it's done right, anyway. It'll give me a chance to look around to see if I can find that damn Q-23 formula."

The two shadowy forms soon left the car and floated toward the warehouse. At the warehouse, they used a crowbar to overpower the lock on the wooden door. Unbeknown to the intruders, this triggered a burglar alarm buzzer located in Kurt Strong's apartment. From Kurt's experience with insurance investigations, he had an intimate knowledge of all types of burglar alarms. When they first set up operations in the warehouse, Kurt considered an alarm connected to a central station or direct to the police, but in the interests of economy, he had it directly connected to his apartment.

Kurt's first reaction was to answer the telephone, but stopped with hand suspended in mid air as he realized this was not the phone ring—but instead was the distinctive buzz of the burglar alarm at the warehouse. Turning off the buzzer, he again turned to the phone and dialed a number. "Roger," said a tense Kurt, "the burglar alarm at the warehouse just went off in my apartment. Now, it may be a false alarm, but I'm going over there to check it out. I'm about ten minutes from the warehouse, so if I don't call you within twenty minutes, you call the police."

Without waiting for a response, Kurt hung up the phone, slipped his revolver in his pocket, started to leave, and went back to his phone. He dialed another number. "Sissy, this is Kurt. This may be a scoop for you, maybe not. The burglar alarm at the plant just went off. I'm going there now, and the police are being notified. If you want to go to the plant, it may be a story. If you do, I'll see you there."

"Thanks, Kurt," she replied. "I'll be there in about half an hour. Be careful."

Back at the warehouse, Sylvester and Dirk were starting to survey the interior with the help of a flashlight.

"Hey," exclaimed Sylvester. "There's a desk and a filing cabinet over in that corner. Hold everything till I take a look for that formula." The beam from the flashlight also showed Sylvester a small desk lamp. "I guess this won't show too much light," he said as he snapped it on. He first went through the desk, scattering papers everywhere. "Damn, nothing here," he groused as he turned his attention to the filing cabinet.

Dirk spoke up. "We better get on the torch job and get the hell out of here."

"Okay," muttered Sylvester, as in the dim light from the desk lamp he surveyed the room. With his flashlight, he pointed to a large object looming on the far side. "Looks like that may be our baby."

They made their way to the object, which turned out to be the batch kettle. "Yeah," said Sylvester. "This must be it. Let me check to see if it's operational." He climbed up the ladder, lifted a corner of the lid, and shone his flashlight down on the mixture inside. An agitator at the bottom of the kettle was gently moving the liquid. For a moment, Sylvester was transfixed by the light on the slow undulations of the pale green, translucent fluid that had caused him so many problems. His eyes glistened fiercely as he stared at this source of his troubles.

A loud, "Hey! Is that it?" from Dirk startled Sylvester, who, from his elevated perch, looked up just in time to see through a window in the warehouse a pair of car headlights pull up outside.

"Quiet," hissed a suddenly alert Sylvester. "Someone's coming. We have to hide."

"Hide!" answered Dirk. "Where the hell are we going to hide? There's no place to hide in here."

Sylvester carefully lowered the lid on the kettle and commanded, "Come up here. We can lie on top of this kettle, and no one can see us from the floor. Hurry up, I hear them at the door."

Sylvester climbed onto the kettle lid and moved to the far side to make room for Dirk, who rapidly climbed the ladder and gingerly crawled out onto the lid. At the same moment, Kurt Strong entered the warehouse with drawn revolver. He had, of course, noted the broken door and the faint light from within, so he knew something was wrong. Kurt flicked the light switch near the door, and the warehouse was flooded with light.

With the sudden flash of light, Dirk, on his knees on the kettle lid, plopped down. The lid on the kettle had been designed to cover the kettle to protect its contents from dust and other contamination, but it was not designed to support the weight of two full-grown men. They could feel the lid giving way, and both emitted howls of terror as they slid into the mixture below them.

Kurt ran to the side of the kettle, and with his revolver covering them, watched the thoroughly drenched, gagging, and completely dejected figures climb out of the kettle and slink down the ladder. They stood beaten and bedraggled under the watchful eye of Kurt, until Roger arrived with Lieutenant Brinkley.

This time there was some real evidence, with the broken lock on the door, the five-gallon can of gasoline, and the two prisoners.

Sissy pulled up in her car a few minutes later. She was met at the door by a policeman, with, "Hey, you can't go in there!"

"But I'm with the *Tribune*," she protested.

"Okay, show me your press card."

"Well, I don't have it with me," Sissy said, justifying it to herself that this was not a lie, but still feeling guilty because she had not yet been made a reporter and therefore did not have a press card.

"You still can't come in without a press card."

Inside, Kurt, who was talking to Lieutenant Brinkley, was keeping an eye out for Sissy, and he heard the policeman at the door. "Lieutenant Brinkley," Kurt motioned toward the door, "I know that girl, and she is with the *Tribune*. How about letting her in?"

"Okay, Sergeant," said the Lieutenant. "She can come in."

Sissy rushed up to Kurt. "Are you all right?"

"Sure I am," reassured Kurt. "In fact, everything is just fine, and do we have a story for you!"

For the next hour, Sissy obtained the facts, and then she rushed to the *Tribune* offices. She was able to write up the story and get it in the next edition as a real scoop.

A few weeks later, Roger and Kurt had just finished a spirited game of tennis at the tennis center and were now seated at the Side Door Bar and Grill, with a glass of beer in front of each of them.

"That was more like it," said Kurt. Roger looked up.

"What was more like it?"

"The tennis," responded Kurt. "That's the first time you gave me a hard time on the courts since you first told me about Q-23, alias Hair-Ban."

Roger smiled. "Well, it's the first time in a while that I've really felt things were in good shape. After the break-in and the contamination from those two characters that fell in my soup, I've been working about forty-eight hours a day to meet the sales commitments you came up with, even with the additional help we hired."

"Actually, I've had to beat off some customers," admitted Kurt. "All the publicity we received from my bride-to-be's articles made my job a snap. Especially the newspaper's pictures of those two in jail the next day with all their hair gone—not just from their heads, but I understand from their entire bodies.

"That was beautiful," gloated Roger. "Just what they deserved. I don't care if they get any prison sentences. That's enough punishment itself, especially for Soly; losing his head of hair really hurt him."

"Well, one thing worries me," said a thoughtful Kurt.

"Yeah, what's that?" asked Roger.

"With you feeling better and better about how things are going, maybe someday you will actually beat me at tennis," said a smiling Kurt.

THE END

About the Author

PAUL R. THEROUX was born the third of Michigan State University engineering professor Frank Theroux's seven children—all of whom went on to graduate from MSU. The professor's love of tennis inspired his children to take up the game also—especially Paul, who not only wound up with shelves full of trophies but also an inspiration for this book, *Q-23*.

Following his years as an Army Air Corps officer in the Pacific during World War II and then as a chemical engineer, Paul entered the fire insurance industry in America, working his way up to executive positions with State Farm and other firms. His marriage to the former Marjorie Withrow resulted in two sons (David and Gary) and a daughter (Linda) who spent their childhoods in a succession of hometowns. The same wanderlust that drove Paul to move his family six times in twenty years really kicked in after he retired—and became a world traveler.

So how does one combine one's fascination with adventure, intrigue, mysteries, travel, and tennis? Well, if you're Paul Theroux, cousin of the novelists Paul, Alexander, and Peter Theroux, you sit down and author this book.

CPSIA information can be obtained at www.ICGtesting.com
Printed in the USA
LVOW06s0723070913

351327LV00001B/3/P

9 780988 655607